This project is sponsored by

Kern County Children
and Families Commission

I0604316

Funded by Proposition 10

THERE'S ONLY ONE OF ME!

by
Pat Hutchins

Greenwillow Books, *An Imprint of* HarperCollins *Publishers*

Pen and ink and felt-tipped markers were used to prepare the full-color artwork.
The text type is Cheltenham.

Library of Congress Cataloging-in-Publication Data

Hutchins, Pat, (date).
There's only one of me! / Pat Hutchins.
p.   cm.
"Greenwillow Books."
Summary: A young girl describes her relationship to the various members of her family,
including her stepfamily, as they all gather to celebrate her birthday.
ISBN 0-06-029819-7 (trade). ISBN 0-06-029820-0 (lib. bdg.)
[1. Family—Fiction. 2. Identity—Fiction.
3. Stepfamilies—Fiction. 4. Birthdays—Fiction.]   I. Title.
PZ7.H96165 Op 2003   [E]—dc21   2002023546

First Edition   10   9   8   7   6   5   4   3   2   1

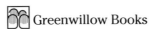

Greenwillow Books

For Stanley Holland Hutchins

I'm my mother's daughter.

I'm my sister's sister.

(AND my mother's daughter, too!)

I'm my half-brother's half-sister.
(AND my mother's daughter
and my sister's sister, too!)

I'm my stepfather's stepdaughter.
(AND my mother's daughter
and my sister's sister
and my half-brother's half-sister, too!)

I'm my stepbrother's stepsister.
(AND my mother's daughter
and my sister's sister
and my half-brother's half-sister
and my stepfather's stepdaughter, too!)

I'm my cousin's cousin.
(AND my mother's daughter
and my sister's sister
and my half-brother's half-sister
and my stepfather's stepdaughter
and my stepbrother's stepsister, too!)

I'm my uncle and aunt's niece.
(AND my mother's daughter
and my sister's sister
and my half-brother's half-sister
and my stepfather's stepdaughter
and my stepbrother's stepsister
and my cousin's cousin, too!)

I'm my grandparents' granddaughter.
(AND my mother's daughter
and my sister's sister
and my half-brother's half-sister
and my stepfather's stepdaughter
and my stepbrother's stepsister
and my cousin's cousin
and my uncle and aunt's niece, too!)

I'm my great-grandmother's great-granddaughter.
(AND my mother's daughter
and my sister's sister
and my half-brother's half-sister
and my stepfather's stepdaughter
and my stepbrother's stepsister
and my cousin's cousin
and my uncle and aunt's niece
and my grandparents' granddaughter, too!)

And I'm a birthday girl today!

(That's a lot of things to be.)

It's nice to be so many things when . . .
there's only
ONE
OF ME!